One Day at a Time

Ramona Golphin-Webb

Copyright © 2018 Ramona Golphin-Webb

All rights reserved.

Published by Stanton Publishing House

Printed in the United States of America

Library of Congress Control Number: 2018962140

ISBN-13: 978-1729031384 (KDP AMAZON)

ISBN-13: 978-1987005349 (BARNES&NOBLES)

One Day at a Time

Acknowledgment

First, I would like to give all honor to my Heavenly Father. I can do nothing without your spirit. In you I live, I move and have my being.

I would like to pay my regards to my loving Parents, Pastors Raymond, and Mary Golphin. Because of you two teaching and showing me the ways of Christ I have grown to have my own relationship with God. Mom you are the most giving and joyful person in the world. Thank you for showing me that the joy of the lord is my strength. Dad, you are my hero, no one works as hard as you. I will never give up because you never gave up. Your investment in me was the greatest gift ever given. I live to make you both proud. I love you both.

I would like to thank my loving in-laws, Bishop Ron Webb, and Dr. Georgia Webb. Both of you pushed me and motivated me to finish the Good work. Just for being a call away for anything I need, I say thank you. Your support and prayers literally birthed this book forth. You two forever hold a special place in my heart.

I wish to present a special thank you to my auntie, Dr. Sharon Nesbitt. Ever since I was 15 you have paved the way for me as an example, a role model, and a finisher. I have watched you live with such integrity and I am confident because of you. I love you.

Thank you, Apostle Resia Thompson. Thank you for speaking truth over my life. Your presence is motivating. You have impacted my life more than you know. I love you.

Crystal, David, Ramira, and Raymond. You all are the wind beneath my wings. I am blessed to have siblings like you. I love you all so much.

Kenyhatta, you helped pull me through. You never let up on me when I would procrastinate. You told me that people were going to hell daily and their blood would be on my hands if I didn't finish this book. I kept that as motivation. Thanks for staying on me about getting this book out. I love you.

Natalie, thank you for being my prayer partner and for holding me accountable. You always give me new perspectives about things. I value your honesty. I Love you.

Preface

This book is based on my obedience and sacrifice to God. I never intended on writing a book. All I wanted to do was encourage others to never give up, hang in there and to trust God. I never considered myself a great writer, but more of a speaker until my mother told me if I could speak, then I could write.

So, I began on social media writing random post encouraging and motivating my friends on Facebook. I didn't think much of it, all I knew was it was a blessing to me so maybe it would help at least one other person. Minutes after I would post a status, my inbox would flood with 'thank you' and "girl I need that's" based off of what I posted. I was shocked, but I still did not consider putting my thoughts and writings in a book. This particular lady sent me an inbox quoting, I love your daily post. Because of your words, I know I can go on. I can forgive and love again. I look forward to reading your writings, I wish they were in a book! At the moment I believed I had something that was bigger than me. God gave me a gift and it was time to share it with the world.

It was time to go beyond social media. I begin to write,

and the rest is history. I pray that this 31-day devotional blesses you beyond measure. My prayer is that each day you

are encouraged, motivated, and pushed. We are so busy that we forget to spend time with God. Knowing how important it is to renew our minds daily to his word, I have decided a 31-day devotional would be the perfect solution. Right before getting out of bed or before closing your eyes, I have written small daily nuggets, prayers, declarations, and confessions to encourage you along the way.

I know this will bless you...

One prayer at a time, one confession at a time, and one powerful devotion at a time...

Remember; never concern yourself with tomorrow or next week; for it will take care of itself.

Trust God... One Day at a Time.

Dedication

Tony, my husband, thank you sweetie for believing in my dreams. Thank you for making it easy for me to obey God. I love you

Finally, I dedicate this book to my greatest investments; Tony Seth Webb and Maleah Crystal-Raye Webb, my heart skips a beat when I look at you both. You two will never know how much I need you and love you. Mommy did it because of you both.

One Day at a Time

Contents

Day 1

A Fresh Start

Isaiah 43:18-19 NIV

18 Forget the former things. Do not dwell on the past.

19 See, I am doing a new thing now it springs up; do you not perceive it? I am making a way in the wilderness and streams in the wasteland.

Today is the perfect day to forget those things of the past. It is a new dawn, a new mercy, but most importantly a fresh start. God promises to make all things new in your life if you can trust him. The scripture commands us to forget the past. It encourages us to never dwell on what happened or what did not happen. Every event, circumstance, or situation is currently outdated and expired. The God of creation is ready to introduce you to a new place of opportunity. God gets joy out of fulfilling his word in our lives. If you can trust him, he promises to do exactly what the scripture reads. He desires to do a new thing in your life. The scripture tells us that he has already made the way so there is no need to doubt or worry. Are you ready to live your best life? Are you able to trust that he can literally change what you feel was a mistake into a miracle? New wells in your life are about to overflow with love, joy, peace, clarity, and provision. God has already made a way in the wilderness and streams in the wasteland. This means that in your time of need and confusion, streams of purpose and provision is already provided. Today is the day to get back on track with God and watch him perform his perfect will in your life. Open the door of faith and encounter the NEW YOU. Be encouraged.

Prayer: God you are the God of a fresh start. My past does not define me, and neither will it hinder me. I am looking forward to a brighter future. No longer will I allow circumstances or past mistakes to keep me from your perfect will. My life is in your hands. Thank you for making all things new. I am ready for my new beginning. In Jesus Name. Amen.

Day 2

A Second Chance

2 Samuel 12:13-14, 24 NIV

13 Then David said to Nathan, "I have sinned against the Lord." Nathan Replied, The Lord has taken away your sin. You are not going to die.

14 But because by doing this you have shown utter contempt for the Lord, the son born to you will die.

24Then David comforted his wife, Bathsheba, and went in unto her, and lay with her: and she bare a son, and he called his name Solomon, and the LORD loved him.

You may feel as if you have messed up so bad that God has left you or forsaken you. I am sure some friends and family have kept a record of all your shortcomings. King David could tell you about a God of a second chance. He like all of us, have made some horrible mistakes and choices. King David coveted another man's wife and got her pregnant. As if that was not enough, he then sent her husband to the front-line of the war to be killed. He attempted to cover up his wrong as if God did not see it. God spared David's life, but he took his first son instead.

Sometimes the consequences of our personal sins effect more than just us. David could have blamed God or cursed God, but he did not. He went to the temple to repent and worship. David, a man after God's own heart made a bad choice but he realized his sin and asked God to forgive him. God forgave David and gave him and Bathsheba another son. They named their son Solomon. Solomon was the wisest man whom ever lived. I like to think that even after David's mistake, wisdom was birthed. God is a God of second chances. Sin has its wage, but God's grace and forgiveness are sufficient. God will give you another chance, just like he did for David. You can repent right now and make things right with him. He is waiting with open arms to receive you. Do not run, do not hide, and do not stay in the mess. Confess your sins to him, turn from your distraction, and prepare yourself for greater. "He is the God of second chances, make it right today."

Prayer: God I know I have made some horrible choices and I have sinned against you. I ask that you forgive me and help me move forward in you. I know you are a God of a second chance. Your word reminds me that no matter what I have done, I can repent and start over again. Thank you for giving me another chance. In Jesus name. Amen.

Day 3

Joy in the Morning

Psalm 30:5 NIV

For his anger lasts only a moment, but his favor lasts a lifetime; weeping may stay for the night, but rejoicing comes in the morning.

Have you ever cried so much that you thought the tears would never stop flowing? Perhaps you were sure that the storms were raging with no relief and no way out? What a great relief it is to know that our tears can only last for so long. I am sure we all have experienced a time where life seemed to suck the hope and joy from within. Those times of midnight will surely happen. We cannot escape them all, but we can learn how to successfully deal with them. We learn through the word of God how to deal with each and every situation. No matter what you may be going through there is nothing that you carry that God cannot handle. He specializes in making ways for you. The truth about trouble is that it can't last always. Weeping, heartache, pain, and discomfort can only last for a season. It is promised that if we faint not, joy will come in the morning. The joy of the Lord is your strength. We can rejoice in the lord through any midnight situation. We have a God that is concerned with whatever saddens us. His word reminds us to receive his Joy. Do not settle for happiness because it depends on what has happened in your life but allow the Joy of the lord to fill your life. When joy is present it remains regardless of what happens. It is a permanent Strength. Declare it now over your day! Today is a day of Joy and strength. So, dry your tears and exit your fears. The God of the universe promises his love, peace, and joy. Wakeup! Joy is here.

Prayer: Lord God, I am trading my sorrow, my pain, and my midnight situations for your joy. I will never be depressed another day in my life. I find my hope and purpose in you. I now receive your strength and your assurance. The Joy you bring is here. I believe it and I receive it. In Jesus name. Amen.

Day 4

Unconditional Love

1 Corinthians 13:4-5 NIV

Love is patient, Love is kind. It does not envy, it does not boast, and it is not proud. It does not dishonor others, it is not self-seeking, it is not easily angered, and it keeps no record of wrongs.

God is love. It is as simple as it reads. His love for us breathes grace, forgiveness, and truth. If you were the only one who needed a savior, he would have still sent his son. Calvary would still be the first date of pure love and truth. God's love for humankind is a love that cannot be defined. It is hard to describe. The closest word to describe it is unconditional. Unconditional love is known as affection without limits and conditions. It is love that thinks of another beyond itself. Did you know that you qualify for this type of love? Today you must know that you are loved with a love that desires nothing from you. His love is a love that is patient, kind, not easy to anger, and one that never keeps a record of wrong. The love God gives goes far beyond any love that you may think you have experienced. No matter who you are and where you are from, it does not matter how you got here or what you have done, Gods love for you is unconditional. All you have to do is receive it and walk in it. God loves you so much that he sent his son to redeem you from sin. Humankind has a love that feels so true at times, but he tends to let you down. Man's definition of love requires so much but gives so little in return. It leaves you empty wanting and longing for more, but with no selfish intent, Gods love surrounds your very being. The Bible says his banner over us is love. Rest in knowing that you are loved by the creator of love himself. Nothing can separate us from the love of God. Because God loved us so much he sent his son that we may have life and life abundantly. Will you receive that love today?

Prayer: Father God, I thank you for your unconditional love that you show me day after day. I know that I am special with nothing to ever separate me from your unconditional love. I need the love that only you give. I accept your love. Amen.

Day 5

Because God is For Us

Romans 8:31 NIV

What then shall we say in response to these things? If God is for us, who can be against us?

I want to encourage you and remind you of the all-powerful, mighty in battle, God that we serve. God is truly on your side. Romans declares that if God is for us, who can stand against us? The answer is no one. For we wrestle not with flesh and blood but with spirits in dark and high places. When a battle presents its self physically you have to fight back spiritually. The battles that we face are not meant to take us out. These battles are to make us strong. God proves himself the more through the victories in our lives. If he does not remove us from the fire, he promises to get in the fire with us. It is one thing to read about all the victories in the bible and all the ways God made; but it is another thing to actually come out of a personal battle, having experienced the hand of God giving you the victory. I want you to know that the fight is inevitable but so is the victory. God is fighting and defending his word in your life. The battles of life are promised to arise so think it not strange when they randomly pop up. As long as we are on this earth we all will be confronted with the adversary. It really does not matter what area he may try to attack or distract, we serve the Lion of Judah. We have A God that promises to stand with us. Even when it seems as if you are sinking or drowning, rest assured knowing that because God is for you, therefore, no other can defeat you. You are not in this fight of life alone. Be encouraged. Jehovah Nissi has already fixed the fight. We win! Keep the faith and finish with the victory.

Prayer: Lord God, my savior, and my protection; I thank you for always having my back. I thank you that your word never fails and neither does your promises. You are for me and the greater one resides in me. I am not afraid or alone. I am victorious through you. Amen

Day 6

Let It Go

1 Peter 5:7 NIV

Cast all your anxiety on him because he cares for you.

This day is already filled with enough worries, to-do's, and concerns. If you are feeling stressed, overwhelmed or overworked you may be overburdened. The Bible tells those who are weary, heavy laden and burdened to come and he will give you rest. The assurance of knowing that God wants us to CAST all of our anxiety, cares and worries upon him is more than a lighter load. It is a complete release from anything that oppresses you or causes you to feel stressed. His yoke is easy, and his burden is light. Life can be so hard sometimes that we begin to carry things within us and on us. We want to figure it and we want to fix it. When we realize that it is too much to carry instead of giving it to God, we continue to load the baggage. Many are depressed, oppressed, and sick because they refuse to LET go and allow God. Today is the best day to release it all to God. Do not worry it, cry about it, or even complain about it. Let It Go. God is ready to relieve you of your pain, grief, stress, and concerns. When you cast your cares upon him the load is lighter immediately. Today will be better than yesterday. All you need to do is open up your heart and release every anxiety or care to him. Do not allow depression to stay. Go now in faith, tread lightly in the trust of a promised peace. The load just lifted, and your best days begins NOW.

Prayer: Lord God Almighty, I give your praise for taking my cares and concerns as your own. I know that when I cast my cares upon you, any stress or anxiety immediately leaves from my life. I now walk in faith and hope. Thank you for always caring for me. Amen.

Day 7

New Mercies

Lamentations 3 :22-23 NIV

22) It is because of the Lord's mercies that we are not consumed, because his compassion fails not.

23) They are new every morning, great is thy faithfulness.

When I think of the mercy that God gives us all daily, my soul is full of joy. Because of his mercy, you have been kept and preserved to finish. His mercies are new every morning, meaning that it is his will to show us his love and compassion beyond our faults and mistakes. Mercy is the compassion or forgiveness shown toward someone whom it is within one's power to punish or harm. This tells us that even when we are guilty his mercy steps in and defends his love. The Bible says that God has mercy on whom he wills. Some people feel that God is a big strong man with a hammer that waits to beat us over the head whenever we fall or sin. In actually he is our father waiting with open arms motioning us to come back home. I am reminded of the story of the prodigal son. The younger son went away and spent his inheritance with riotous living later to return to his father house. When his father saw him from afar he met him, hugged him and threw the biggest welcome home party ever. I am sure the son contemplated several times returning home, but he thought that perhaps his father would not receive him. Just as his father embraced him and showed him mercy, our heavenly father awaits our arrival. Run to the mercy seat. Never stay away because of how you were living or what you have done. His mercies are new every day. God knew we would need his grace and mercy.

Great is the faithfulness of our heavenly father. It is his heart's desire that no man perish, no man hurts or lacks. Will you receive his forbearance today? He is waiting.

Prayer: God, I thank you for your mercy and your grace. Because of your love for me, I will never be consumed. You always prepare a way of escape. I thank you for saving me from the snares and traps the enemy intended to destroy me with. Great is your mercy towards me. Amen.

Day 8

Nothing is Impossible with God

Mark 9:23 NIV

Jesus said unto him, "If thou can't believe, all things are possible to him that believeth."

I am so glad that the God I serve specializes in what we call (impossible) solutions. He loves to flex his glory in areas that we cannot fix ourselves. Could you just hand over your life? Hand over your worries, fears, mistakes, and belongings? No problem is too big that he cannot hold. Too short that he cannot reach. Too damaged that he cannot restore. Too broken that he cannot repair. Too much that he cannot manage or to messed up that he cannot redeem. He is the potter, you are the clay. Allow him to make and mold you. You cannot handle life continual blows. You can try but eventually, you will become weary and worn out. He is waiting to restore, love and repair your life. Nothing is impossible to those who believe.

Hannah was barren but believed and God gave her a son.

Enoch believed God and was taken to heaven without dying.

Noah believed God and built a large boat to save his family from a flood he had never seen before.

Abraham prepared in obedience to slay Isaac as a sacrifice, but he fully believed that God would either resurrect his son Isaac from the dead or provide another sacrifice.

What are you believing God for? The Bible says if you can believe and have no doubt in your heart, believe you will receive, and it will be yours. You can speak to this mountain and it will be removed. You do not have to climb the rough side of the mountain any longer. Just believe. What mountains are in your life that seems like they will not move? Today you have the power to speak to them and watch them be moved and cast away. Nothing is impossible with God.

Prayer: Father God, I come before you, thanking you for your faithfulness. I believe your word. I trust your word. Nothing is impossible because I believe. Today is my day of faith. I trust you with all of me. Amen.

Day 9

Bulldog – Faith

Personal Testimony

The just shall live by faith.

Today I want to encourage you to keep the faith. I would like to share one of the most trying times in my life.

I remember receiving a heart-breaking report from my doctor. The report was unexpected, devastating, and seemed unfair. I needed the comfort that only God could give. I knew I could either continue to cry my eyes out or I could get up and fight. So that is exactly what I did. I began to dry my eyes and plead my case to God. I told him, "God all I have is my faith, all I have is my hope; I need a creative miracle." Later that evening I remember expressing the results with a few of my faith-filled friends and immediate family members.

Never share the news that requires crazy faith to just anybody. Some of them will talk you right into doubt. Make sure they are faith-filled and that they to believe that God

WILL Do It.

Back to the story:

My faith-filled few made me feel encouraged, yet, and still, I knew that I needed a creative miracle. They promised to pray but I knew I had a real fight on my hands. I had to fight the good fight of faith. I walked upon a true test of faith and this was the moment to either hold or to fold. Everything I heard in church, all I have read, all I have written and spoken became the true test. The test to see the weight of my own faith.

It is one thing for others to pray, but you to have a measure of faith. Sarah at the age of 90, was able to conceive a son because of HER faith. Everything possible said NO until she believed herself. It was HER OWN faith that enabled her to birth a promise. A promise she named (ISSAC).

Back to the Story:

The thoughts began to invade my mind, "Did I just proclaim, keep the faith," over others and could not apply it over my own life? All of these thoughts, emotions, and perceptions came to my mind. I knew what I needed to do. I begin to confess God's promises through his word. I began lifting myself from doubt to fully believing God could and he would hear my cry. I began confessing his word over my situation.

I said things like...

God nothing is impossible with you

You are a miracle worker

The fruit of my womb is blessed and abundant

My seed is mighty in the earth

I trust you God with my life

I will not faint but see the manifested promise.

You know the plans you have for me, they are good, and they are not to harm me.

It was vital for me to have God's word in my heart. When the adversary came with a thought of Doubt, I came with the word of God.

(I would google stories of success from other women who received the same news that I had received. If the story seemed like the results were not what I was believing for, I would stop reading it and find another success story. Everything I read, watched and listened to had to be in alignment with what I was believing God for.)

Faith comes by hearing and hearing and hearing, and hearing and hearing the word of God. When you continually hear the word, it becomes alive. You then have the substance to move upon. Faith without YOUR MOVEMENT is dead.

I knew all I needed at that time was stories of how God made a way where the doctors and nurses could not see the way.

My mental atmosphere completely changed.

The just shall live by faith.

I was reminded of the bulldog. The bulldog gets a grip on what he wants and does not let go until he has it. Some say they can still breathe while biting. Bulldog faith is grip holding with no intention of fainting until the hope for substance is in possession. That is my definition.

I wrote this to tell you that this is exactly what happened to me........

I went back to the doctor and he informed me that my lab results showed that I had a possible blighted ovum. A blighted ovum meant that a gestational sac was present, but the embryo did not form. Basically, saying that I had a chemical pregnancy and he did not see a baby nor a trace of a heartbeat. He said I am going to give you one more ultrasound but after this, I would be scheduled to have the sac removed.

I had gone through labs and test for several weeks now

and I could not accept being pregnant and not giving birth!!!!!! He went ahead with the ultrasound. I immediately begin to pray within myself! A few seconds later, my faith manifested a miracle. A miracle of life, in fact, that precious miracle continued to grow inside of me. I remember hearing a thumping strong heartbeat. I cried like a broken cookie!!!! I was so happy!! Six months later, I gave birth and I named her Maleah Crystal-Raye Webb. God is Faithful! God is still in control no matter what man predicts. God is all knowing, all-seeing, and most of all, he is the giver of good gifts.

I hope I encouraged you in some way. Today was not a devotional but more of the testimony of the goodness of the lord. Keep the faith and manifest your heart's desire. I am a Witness!

Get a bulldog grip on it, meaning breath while you're biting! Do not let go or let up until it manifest.

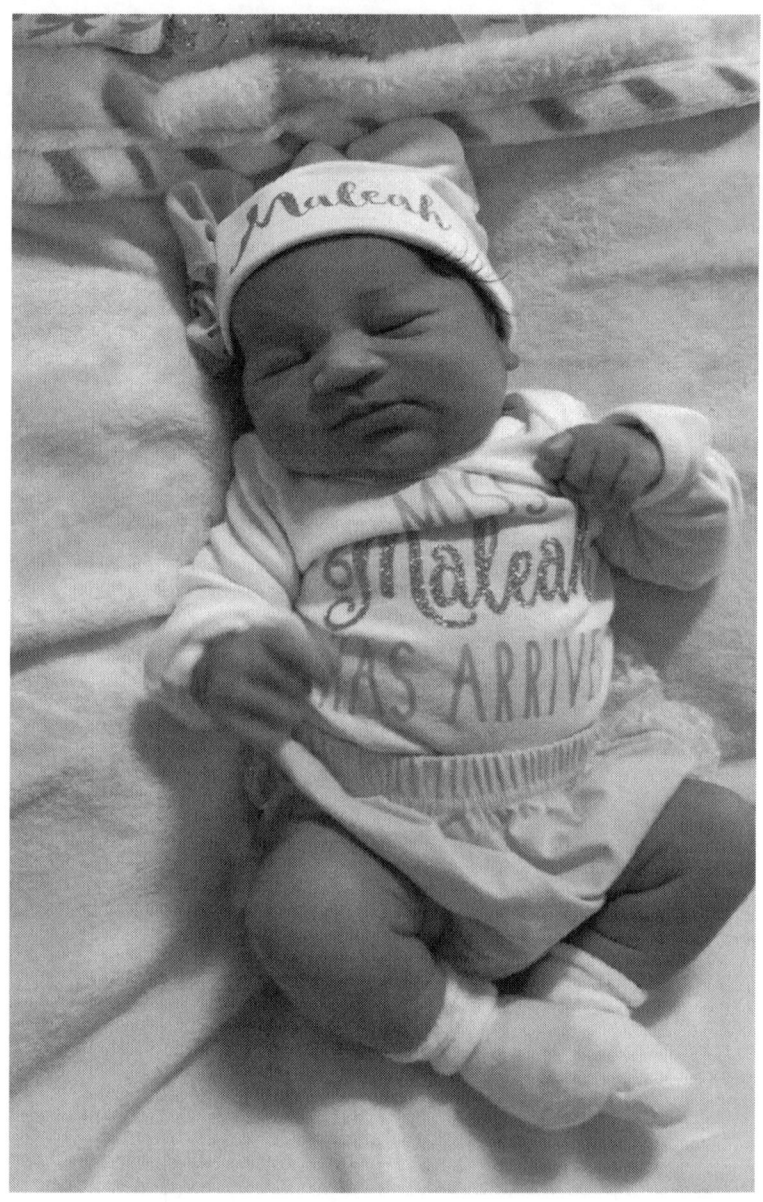

Maleah Crystal-Raye Webb
Born: 8/28/18

Day 10

"'Tis so sweet to Trust"

Proverbs 3:5-6 NIV

Trust in the Lord with all your heart and lean not to your own understanding but in all your ways acknowledge him and he shall direct your paths.

I'm sure you have heard the old song," Tis so sweet to Trust in Jesus," just to take him at his word. Just to rest upon his promise. Every time I hear it, or I read the lyrics of this song my concerns vanish. It is so much peace in knowing that when you have full trust in God the days get sweeter. When was the last time you checked the screws or legs on a chair before you sat down? I am sure you do not because you trusted that the chair would hold. You have flopped down in many chairs before that have held you, so you automatically, unknowably have trust that all chairs can hold you without breaking. Why don't we trust in God to keep us, hold us and to instruct our lives as we trust in a chair? His capacity and ability to hold you and keep you goes far be-yond that of a chair. Naturally, when we become weighted, certain chairs will collapse if you attempt to have a seat in them, but spiritually no matter what you have lost or baggage that has accumulated, God still has the ability to hold you. You just have to trust him. The song goes on to say, "Just to rest upon his promise." Have you ever just needed rest within your thinking or in your soul? Sleep is one thing, but rest is another. The body can be sleep, but if worry, doubt, and concern are in your soul it is hard to truly rest.

I am writing this to encourage you that God wants you to lean and depend on him. Many lean on God but do not fully depend on him. He is asking for you to fully trust him. Fully leaning and depending on him for everything. He has the rest that your soul desires. It is deeper than a newborn ba-bies' slumber. It is a rest where your burdens are lifted, and your mind is clear. When we put our trust in Jesus he then has the control over our circumstances. There is no need to hold on to anything while trusting him. Our belief in him causes doubt to become faith. Knowing that you do not have to do anything in this life in your own strength is enough to make you want to serve God. It makes you want to praise him and thank him for allowing us to cast all of our cares upon him because he cares for us. That includes every concern, worry, doubt, and anything else that bothers you. Cast it to the one who can carry it. He knows what you are going through and desires to lift every heavy burden. For his yoke is easy and his burden is light! Hand it over today, he is waiting for you to trust him with all you have and all you are!

Remember, one day at a time. One step at a time. Trust him.

Prayer: God I am learning how to fully put my trust in you. From this day forward, I am leaning and depending on you. I will trust in you with all my heart, mind, and soul. Amen.

Life is to Short

Maximize the Moment

Give your Best

Today will never happen again so make it count.

Ramona Golphin-Webb

Day 11

Stay focused!

Proverbs 4:25 AMP

Let your eyes look directly ahead, and your gaze be fixed straight before you.

Hey you! Yes you, right here. I know your phone just got an email, the toast just popped up and the washer just sang a song of completion. But can you focus in on what you are reading without giving in to distraction?

It can be a challenge. We all have such busy lives. We have so much to do and so many people depending on us that it becomes difficult to stay focused. Staying focused is different than to just focus. It is easy to begin a thing, the work comes when you have to really concentrate, dive in, tune in, and block out the surroundings and continue until finished.

The scriptures tell us to keep focused on the goal! It tells us that commitment is the assurance of a clear vision. I rejoice in knowing that God makes the blur fade when we focus in with full dedication. He promises us to make the path straight if we can just stay on task. Have you ever gotten lost or missed an exit because you were on the phone or your child or friend had your attention? I am sure we all have. Then you have to take an alternate route to get back on track. It is more time, gas, energy, and headache when we lose focus from our ultimate plan or destination. You can definitely get back on track but now the finish is prolonged! Here comes traffic! Here comes frustration! Our goal today is to stay focused to finish. Let us tune in like never before on the things that God has for us. His plan is that we prosper and succeed. His will is that we win and triumph. We can only get his best if we master the skill of staying focused. We must remain unwavering, unmovable, and un-distracted, like an eagle's eye after its prey! Nothing will ever take the eye of an eagle from his prey. His focus is so locked in that he would die before taking his eye off his prey! Let us learn from the eagle! Stay focused and keep striving. If you have given in to distraction, make today a new start. Take it one day at a time, focusing on a few things to assure a strong finish! Be blessed, and remember, take it one day at a time!

Prayer: Lord I now understand how important it is to stay focused. I am now more focused than I have ever been. I want what you have already designed for me. I know in order to receive and produce excellence I need to stay focused. My focus is on you. My eyes are on the prize. Forgive me for focusing on other things and being so busy doing my own thing. I have gotten off in many areas, but today I made a decision to keep the main things, the main things. I thank you for revealing to me what I should be doing. You have my undivided attention. Amen.

Remember Gods Principles and

Relax in his Promises

No matter what may happen, Rest assured that

God already knows, and he is in Control.

Relax &Remember

One day at A Time

Ramona Golphin-Webb

Day 12

For all have sinned

Romans 3:23 KJV

For all have sinned and come short of the glory of God.

The Bible clearly tells us in scripture that we have all sinned, meaning we have all missed the mark. The greatest example to me was, if we all attempted to throw a rock to China, I am sure many of your rocks would land a lot further than mine. With China being the mark, I know for a fact that all of us did not make it. Our rocks landed different place, some further than others but no one's rock actually landed in China.

This example is a clear view of what the scripture is saying to us. No matter who you are, where you come from, what position you hold, or the dollar amount in your bank account; you have missed the mark at some point. This is not to discourage you, but to remind you that you are not alone. You are not the only person that has blown it. We have all made mistakes that we are not proud of. We have all sinned against God, therefore, we should not judge anyone. The amazing thing about God is that he knew our rocks would never make it to China. He knew we would slip and fall. Because of his love for us, he sent his son to redeem us from sin. Jesus Christ shed his blood so that I never have to fault myself for falling short. All we have to do is accept him as our savior and lord. At that moment we hand over our rocks and began to stand on the rock of our salvation. On Calvary, he threw a rock that landed far beyond China's wall. He did that for you and for me. So today, thank him for redeeming you. Thank him for giving you another chance to make the mark. We press for the mark of the high calling in and through Jesus Christ! Be blessed and be encouraged!

Prayer: Father God, oh how we love you. We adore the love you have shown us. Your action of love and grace covered our shortcomings. Because of you only, are we able to stand boldly and declare the victory. Our mark is made in you and only through you. We no longer see our inadequacy or deficiencies. You hold our hands and live in our hearts. We are forever grateful. Let us never forget the price you paid and the position you played.

We are forever indebted! Amen!

Day 13

Nothing but the Blood

Hebrews 9:14 NIV

How much more, then will the blood of Christ, who through the eternal spirit offered himself unblemished to God, cleanse our consciences from acts that lead to death, so that we may serve the living God.

What can wash away my sins? Nothing but the Precious Blood of Jesus.

What picks me up and carries me when I fall? Nothing but the blood of Jesus. The most important thing in life is to understand why Jesus shed his blood and to believe that he did if for the redeeming of humankind. Do you know that his blood was shed because he loved you knowing that you fall, sin, curse him, doubt him, and deny him? Yet and still he died anyway. What an amazing love. Who could you think of that would give their life for you knowing that you would take their love and sacrifice for granted? Who would shed their blood knowing that you did not believe in them?

That answer is Jesus Christ. Over 2,000 years ago he made the ultimate sacrifice to give up his life so that you and I may live. Not only live, but to live with purpose and to a life of abundance. Until you get the revelation of his Blood you will merely exist, but you will never be able to truly live the abundant life. Because of his blood, we never have to accept sickness, depression, oppression, lack, sin, or anything contrary to his word. All of those things fall under his blood. His blood does not cover our sins, but it wipes them away as if they had never existed. The blood is so powerful that it speaks on your behalf. In the bible days, the Israelites were commanded by Moses to slang the blood on their door post. At the time they were in Pharaoh's bondage and Gods last plague was about to come upon the land. It was the death of the firstborn whose house did not have the blood on the door post. The death angel would come by and when he saw the blood, he would pass by. When the death angel showed up, the family did not have to speak, pray, sing, or peek out the window. Having the blood on the doorpost spoke life over the entire house. Death saw the blood and had to Passover. That representation of the Blood still speaks today. Back in Moses days, they used the blood of an animal to represent the sacrifice of Jesus Christ but today the Blood of Jesus Christ has been shed. We do not need the blood of a bull, goat, or lamb. Jesus came and shed his blood once and for all. That same bloodshed over 2,000 years ago SPEAKS on the behalf of those who apply it today. If you have accepted and confessed with your mouth, Christ as your personal savior, believing that he died and rose, then you are an applicant of the blood. Apply the blood over your mind, home, business, children, job, body and bank accounts. Nothing but the blood! Remember the price that was paid for you. Apply the blood of Jesus today.

Take a moment to thank God for the blood of Jesus.
Thank him in your own way.

Don't overdo it

Don't over think it

Settle it and Believe in your heart

One Day at A Time

Ramona Golphin-Webb

Day 14

When I Die, I want to Die Emptied, Not Just Old

Jeremiah 29:11 NIV

For I know the plans I have for you, "Declares the Lord, "plans to prosper you and not to harm you, plans to give you a hope and a future.

The cemetery is the wealthiest place in the world. The reason that it is so wealthy is that many people died with gifts, talents, books, businesses, solutions, ideas, and inventions. Have you ever wondered if some of the cures and answers the world is looking for are buried in the grave? Or perhaps they are still locked up inside of you?

We have put the emphasis on dying at an old age but forgot that the true reason for dying is because we have fully emptied ourselves of everything given. Many have died with wealth locked up on the inside of them. We search year after year, state after state, validation after validation for the very thing that was inside of us all along. Some have died with the very essence of their existence because they did not dis-cover their gift, or they were:

Afraid to TRY

Afraid to FAIL

Afraid of what others would think or say

We have to understand that we are gifted for a reason. The GIFT is waiting to be opened and displayed. We all have different gifts, and some have more than others. Do not worry about that it is perfectly on purpose for a purpose. Just because you have 2 and your neighbor has 5 does not mean that your two are less important or less valuable. DO YOU!

Remember, "too much GIVEN; MUCH is required!"

For an example; let us just think about the human body. It has several different functions / parts but one whole body working together as one. That is exactly how our gifts work! No one was left out! We all have a reason to live and a greater reason to die.

There is no need to die prematurely, commit suicide or feel insignificant. We must simply take time with our selves; no television, no cell phones, and just think quietly and med-itate on why we are here. Dig within yourself to discover your true importance. Ask GOD to show you! Once you have discovered it, you will then experience the greatest Joy and a perfect Peace.

My father always said, "The greatest tragedy is not dying, its dying and never finding and fully finishing the reason for your existence." Pastor Raymond Golphin

Let us make up our minds to die emptied and not just OLD. We can start today by utilizing everything possible that has already been given to us. It is our job to discover that hidden thing that no man can fire us from or take from us. The world is waiting, and your PEACE depends on it.

A great man once said, "They can't fire you from Your GIFT." The business could close today but a person who knows their gift will always make it. Do not add more value to your grave; add the value to your life!

Prayer: Lord I am grateful for the plans you have for me. Your word tells me to submit my plan to you and you will bring success. My success is through you. I submit my work to you today.

It may not look like it

May not seem like it but keep moving forward

The destination is closer than you think

The race is not given to the swift, but to those

Who endure to the finish

Don't faint, Keep Going

Ramona Golphin-Webb

Day 15

4 key P's to Success

Proverbs 16:13 NIV

Commit to the Lord whatever you do, and he will establish your plans.

Every human being was born with a particular passion and goal. We also have a hunger to accomplish something in our lifetime. We all have the same beginning, but only a few of us finish because we do not maximize these 4 Steps. These easy keys will push you into destiny. They are 100% guaranteed when utilized correctly!

Let us begin

1. **Pray**- it is simply talking to God. The one who gives success. Pray and allow God to lead you in the right direction. Pray that you meet the right people at the right time in the right place. Pray and believe what you pray. Allow him to lead and guide your footsteps. Pray the prayer of FAITH. You will need to be sure that what you are wanting is really what you should be trying to achieve. You will find that out

through prayer. It is simple. Ask him.

2. **Perception** -Perception is the state or process of being aware, alert, the full ability to hear and see. It is important to have a clear Perception of knowing that you can have what you see and if you fully believe, based on your opinion of the matter. You have to change the way you view the mountain in order to conquer it. It is all about how you perceive yourself! Have you seen your self-celebrating at the finish line? Change your negative, limited thinking and think BIG! Think as a finisher. So as a man thinks, so is he!

3. **Preparation** – the act or process of making ready for consideration or use. Everybody wants to be a millionaire, but ask yourself, am I really ready to be a millionaire? What would be the purpose of me being one? Could you even count it? I am saying this to say it is important to be ready and prepared for success. Get your affairs in order. Prepare your mind for creative thinking, your body for long hours and not as much sleep, your soul for a passion that drives you daily. Get ready for it! Research, talk with others who have already mastered where you want to go; so, when your time comes it doesn't overtake you or it doesn't ruin you. Ask questions! But most importantly. Be prepared!

4. **Persistence** to continue steadfastly especially in spite of opposition, remonstrance, and difficulties. Push through!

This is major! Stay with it! Do not give up no matter how hard it gets. It will not be easy, but it will be worth it. Stay consistent and do not let anything stop you. Get a bulldog grip on it, meaning breath while you're biting! Do not let go or let up until it manifest. Pursue until it's possessed!

You are on your way! You have four keys … all of them together unlock the door to Success! Apply them one day at a time.

Prayer: Lord I am grateful for the plans you have for me. Your word tells me to submit my plan to you and you will bring success. My success is through you. I submit my work unit our perfect will. I am now ready to see what you have in store for me. My life changes today. Amen.

It may not happen today it may not happen to-morrow, but if you remain diligent and deter-mined... it WILL happen One Day at A Time

Ramona Golphin-Webb

Day 16

The "U" in Unique

Psalms 139:14 KJV

I will praise thee; for I am fearfully [and] wonderfully made: marvelous [are] thy works; and [that] my soul knoweth right well.

Did you know that there is no other creature, being, thing, image, or person like YOU?

"U" were created specifically on purpose for a purpose and with purpose. My father always preached this from the pulpit to our kitchen table. Little did I know how important that statement would be to me. I did not even think about what it really meant; I just thought it was a nice saying. The light bulb popped on. I discovered that I was unique, and I had my own purpose. Purpose to be here; made on purpose and had an even greater purpose to fulfill!

Don't you see the "U" in PURPOSE?? It is intentionally there. Sometimes we feel as if the significance of our being is invalid and overlooked. The truth of the matter is we have failed to see what really sets us apart and makes us individually UNIQUE. Everybody has a deep treasure. The world is in need of that unique thing that only you possess. We need that unique purpose that you hide from us. The world needs that thing that you feel that is not as important. That thing that only you can do it as you do it.

THAT THING!

Did you know that no other human has the same fingerprint as you? That means even your touch is different. Everything you touch will leave with a different imprint. Did you know that no matter how hard we try, we could never be anybody else but our Unique self? You can practice and mimic someone else, but your soul will never be satisfied because even it knows that you are a Created Original.

We get caught up following this trend that trend. We want our bodies to look like this model and we desire to have hair and skin like that person, not knowing that while you are wanting to be like someone else, the next person is wishing to be like you.

How can we fix this identity crisis?

"BE YOU!" Never allow yourself to be compared to anybody or anything.

There are things so unique and different about you if you would just look deeper within. There are things that you can do better if you would allow yourself to become inspired from within first and then out. Do not get me wrong. There are several great role models in the world. Several people to look up too but never to look so far up at them that you begin to look down upon yourself.

You were created to bloom from the inside out. Everything you need you already have. It is uniquely placed in you. You just have to discover it and use it. Look for the U in Unique.

Look in the mirror and say these words...

You want to know what makes you so grand?

You want to know why you do not fit in and why you look the way you do?

It is because there is no another person breathing Gods great air that is more important, more handsome, beautiful, inspiring, intelligent, and unique as YOU! Then strike your most fierce pose and take a Selfie!

Remember the "U" in unique and the "U" in purpose is there for a reason. Shine on!

Today instead of praying, lets practice spiritual exercise. I want you to take a picture of yourself and admire Gods creation. You are something to look at. If God carried a wallet he would have your picture in it; so, smile large, and Walk tall. You are fearfully and wonderfully made.

Dream Big

*It's ok to dream, but don't forget to WAKE up
and make it a reality. See it and Seize it.*

Ramona Golphin-Webb

Day 17

The Man in the Mirror

Romans 8:28 NIV

And we know that in all things God works for the good of those who love him, who have been called according to the purpose.

One of the most difficult things to do is to take a look in the Mirror of life. Rather this mirror is handed to you, given to you or you decided to pick it up and take a glimpse, it can be difficult. It is not that the Mirror is so heavy that you cannot bear it or lift it; it is the fact that once you actually see yourself it is then no excuse for not making the proper changes. Change is not always easy and sometimes it hurts. You have to adapt to it, you have to want it, but first, you must take ownership of what you see. We are not expected to be perfect but through the flaws to become wiser, stronger, and determined to become better. It is so much easier to get upset with who handed us the mirror or who really showed

us ourselves then to actually look and take the full responsi-
bility for our choices, decisions and now consequences. It
has always been easier to point a finger at who was not there,
who left, who did not support, or who hurt you. When will
you move beyond what was done to you and toward what is
in store for you? When can you look in the mirror taking the
good with the bad and saying, yes, I am flawed but I am
moving forward in forgiveness, peace, joy, love, and
purpose. For in all things God works it out for the good.

You can be free today. Today is the day of a complete
healing from your past. I know you may hurt because sometimes the mirror shows things that you had no control over.
It shows those who were supposed to be there but instead
caused hurt and disappointment. I am not saying you blame
yourself for those events, but I am encouraging you to move
past them and use them as motivation. Use them as stepping
stones to a new beginning, a new you, a mind of clarity a
heart of freedom. Free to love, Free to forgive, free to heal.
Do not be afraid of what you may see today. As you take a
self-evaluation please do not become guilty or regretful. Ask
the Holy Spirit to show you and help you deal with the blem-
ishes and scars. He that is in Christ Jesus is a new creation,
the old has become new. Make a decision today to deal with
self-first and allow self to become better first. Look in the

mirror but do not stay there. Make the change one day at a time. It is working for your good now.

Prayer: God I thank you for the person I see in the mirror. I no longer hold anybody in un-forgiveness or bitterness because of my life or what has happened or the choices that I have made. I ask for your forgiveness. Forgive me as I forgive myself. Show me how to let go and allow you to fix what I have flawed and the hurt that others have caused me. Give me the strength to hold my mirror before me in expectation of change and freedom. I thank you right now that I am free from my hurts, my shortcomings, and my past and from people! Amen!

Get back up

Try again

It's going to work this time.

Ramona Golphin-Webb

Day 18

The Guided Path

Psalm 119:105 NKJV

Your word is a lamp to my feet and a light to my path.

I remember going to vacation bible school and learning Psalms 119:105 through a song. The scripture was easy to learn because the music was fun, and they showed us the sign language as well. I enjoyed it because it was catchy and interesting. I had no true idea what this scripture really meant until years later my mother, Pastor Mary, preached a sermon about the context of this scripture. Back in the Bible days, the people would travel with 2 clay lamps. They would wrap a small lamp around their ankles, so they could see directly in front of them and another hand-held clay lamp to see ahead of them.

The small lamp around the ankle helped them prevent stumbling, falling, and potholes. This foot lamp describes the word of God. Thy word is a lamp unto my feet meant that Gods word sheds lights to prevent falling, stumbling and potholes in life. His Word sheds light directly in front of us assuring our safety and promised destiny. The scripture then says, "That the word of God is also a light unto my path." This part of the scripture means that the word of God also secures the future. When you swing the lamp of God's word before you, you can rest assured his guidance. God never promises to show us what is around the corner, but he wants us to trust him step by step and through his word. We do not have to be afraid. No need to worry about tomorrow, next week or next year. Allows Gods word to be a lamp unto your feet and a light unto your path.

Prayer: God I thank you for your word. Your word secures my present and my future. I will not be afraid of what may come or what already is. For your word guides me and will continue to make my path straight. Amen

Day 19

Let us Declare and Confess

HEALING DECLARATION

Isaiah 53:5 KJV

But he was wounded for our transgression, he was bruised for our iniquities: the chastisement of our peace was upon him; and with his stripes we are healed.

It is the will of the father that my body, mind, and emotions be completely healed.

Every system of my body works the way God has intended for it to function.

My circulatory, respiratory, digestive, excretory, nervous, and endocrine system is whole and works effectively.

My immune, integumentary, skeletal, muscle and reproductive systems functions as GOD has created it to do so.

Every cell, blood vessels, platelet, and tissue function according to its created purpose.

My heart, lungs, liver, and kidneys are free from disease.

My body lacks nothing it needs to function properly.

I am not medication dependent.

I am healed from the top of my head to the soles of my feet.

For it is written; your wish for me above all things is that my

souls prosper as well as my body to be in perfect health.

No sickness or disease can survive in my body.

By your stripes, I am healed, delivered, and set free.

Thank you, God, for being my healer! Amen.

Day 20

Strength in the Midst of the Storm

Psalms 46:1-3 NIV

God is our refuge and strength, an ever-present help in trouble.

Today we will focus on taking authority over negative thoughts that come to your mind and finding the strength to do so in the midst of the storm. Everyone has experienced stinking thinking some time in life. It is a natural feeling to feel inadequate or to feel like we just do not have what it takes to make it, especially when going through a storm. This is why it is so important to see and think supernaturally. The Bible tells us to cast down vain imagination. That means that when you have a thought that is negative or against what the word says about you; to immediately send that thought away. Do not even allow yourself to ponder on those thoughts even while the storm is raging. You have to Trash them as soon as they come. Sometimes the storm blurs your vision and alters your thinking because it came unexpected or has caused tremendous damage. I am here to let you know that God is your strength and refuge in times of trouble. Many people try to clear the storm on their own. They wonder why they are so consumed, mentally tired, physically strained, and depressed. Negative thinking feeds from when you are trying to figure out your life on your own. When you cannot figure out what is next or what to do you begin to have thoughts of defeat and feelings of weakness. Truth is you have to align your thinking with what the word says about you.

In our own strength we truly do not have what it takes, but in our weakness, God becomes the needed strength. So please, do not be so hard on yourself. We were created to depend on the creator. Don't go through it alone. His Shelter is available. Call on the Red Cross! That is why once we renew our mind daily to the word of God, we become empowered and nothing is impossible. Once our mind is renewed then our thoughts began to change. When our thinking changes, our actions, motives, and environments change! Shelter takes place! Remember, you can only get these results when you begin to dig in the word of God and learn about who you truly are. So as a man thinks in his heart, so is he! Change your thoughts and watch your life follow.

Prayer: Your word is my strength and my refuge. I align my thoughts with your word, therefore, I do not have to do anything in my own strength. Your word says that you are my help in times of trouble. I receive your shelter in the storm. My thinking changes today. Amen

There is power in No

It's ok to Use it.

Ramona Golphin-Webb

Day 21

Walking After the Flesh

Romans 8:1-2 KJV

There is therefore now no condemnation to those who are in Christ Jesus, who[a] do not walk according to the flesh, but according to the Spirit. 2 For the law of the Spirit of life in Christ Jesus has made me free from the law of sin and death.

The Bible tells us to walk after the spirit and not our flesh. The spirit has made us free from the law of sin and death. Sin always looks good, smells good, feels good but never is good for you. Have you ever heard of "Fool Gold?" It looks like gold, feels like gold but it is not what it seems to be. It has no value. Its agenda is to fool you as if it is real gold. Walking after the flesh is the same exact thing. It feels good, looks good but in the end, it fools you. The flesh will lead you places you never intended. Feeding it and yielding to it leads to the destruction of our bodies and our minds! The bible says that there is nothing good in the flesh, so when you walk after it you are heading down a road of destruction.

We must run from fleshly desires! The Bible tells us that God has prepared an escape for any temptation of the flesh. It is up to us to want to flee. It is not that God does not want us to enjoy life or have fun, it that what he considers sin harms us, hurts us and he wants to prevent that. A good father will always want what is best for his children. The flesh always craves what feels good, looks good and then it gratifies itself until it entangled you, traps you and causes you to become distant from God and full of guilt. It ALWAYS ALWAYS plans to make a fool out of you! My Dad would always tell us that sin will take you further than you wanted to go, make you pay more than your intended to pay and make you stay longer than you intended to stay. Save yourself the frustration, delay, and pain. Make a decision to walk after the Spirit.

Prayer: Forgive me for walking after my own fleshly desires. I have been doing things my way which is unpleasing to you. Today I make a choice to follow your spirit. Amen.

Day 22

Declare and Decree/ I AM

To declare means to proclaim boldly, announce officially, broadcast, and to make an affirmed acknowledgment. Today is a day of declaration and affirmation. Say these declarations aloud.

1. I am the beloved of Christ!
2. I am fully persuaded
3. I am a money magnet
4. I am talented and creative
5. I am healthy and wealthy
6. I walk after the spirit
7. I am an overcomer
8. I am a kingdom financier
9. God can use me
10. I am here on purpose and for a purpose
11. My family is blessed
12. My focus is clear
13. I will never be depressed another day in my life
14. I cannot give up

15. I am anointed

16. I am a billboard for Christ

17. I am delivered

18. My words are powerful

19. God is my source

20. I easily forgive

21. I am success

22. The Holy Spirit is my guide

23. I bear fruit

24. My children call me blessed

25. I live by faith

26. I walk in love

27. I have an appetite for God's word

28. My marriage is affair proof

29. I am favored by God

30. I am a peacemaker

31. I am diligent

32. I am a good Steward of my time and my money

33. My seed is mighty

34. I am forgiven

35. I win

Day 23

Maintenance of the Blessing

Proverb 10:22 NIV

The blessing of the Lord brings wealth without painful toil for it.

Have you ever told a person that God blessed you with something or someone and then something seemed to go wrong with the blessing? Everything seemed to be going great then boom, you begin to question if this thing you labeled a blessing was really from God. What is a blessing? A blessing is Gods favor and protection. When a blessing is placed on a person, marriage, car, or job, then those things are called BLESSED. Have you ever faced these questions? I thought my relationship, my marriage, my new home, my business; the list goes on, was a blessing from GOD? I thought he blessed it! I thought God approved it? We were both equally yoked? This job was my dream job. So why didn't it work? All of these thoughts and questions come to mind when the blessing comes with some maintenance.

There is work for you to do as well. Allow me to help you understand.

If God gives you a brand new, beautiful, fully loaded car and you never get the oil changed, never rotate the tires, never add brake Fluid, never wax it, or clean it? Do you think that the car will function to its created potential? What exactly can you expect from this CAR? So, do/did you really plan to have this CAR a long time? What if you drove reckless and you totaled the car? Whose fault is that? Is it that the car was not a blessing or the person that was given the car did not do the proper maintenance to maintain the blessing? There are blessings that are sent in the form of people, jobs, and opportunities that are God sent that come with maintenance. Your faith even comes with maintenance. It only grows by hearing the word and with YOU moving on the word so what makes you think that when God blesses you with something you will not have to have a proper stewardship to keep it. Please remember God has a part and so do you. The blessings that God gives us do not lead to painful toil. You maintain his blessings through prayer, giving and obedience. He always honors stewardship.

So, my question again. Is it that God did not give it to you? Is it God did not Bless it?

Or was it, YOU did not take care of what God gave you...?

Hmmmm, Selah think on it... Let us Pray

Prayer: Lord God, the giver all good gifts I know that you give blessings that add no sorrow. I now understand how important it is to never take for granted what you have blessed me with. I thank you for your protection and favor. I will do the proper maintenance on what you have given to me. I am grateful. Amen.

I decree this is the year of the Kingdom Financier. God can trust me with Money.
I am a money magnet. I am a 100% tither. I am a good steward of money. I am blessed in the city and the field. I am being blessed in my coming and in my going. I am blessed to be a blessing.

Ramona Golphin-Webb

Day 24

The Battle of the Mind

Philippians 2:5 KJV

Let this mind be in you, which was also in Christ Jesus.

The hardest battle you will ever face is that of the mind. That space in between two ears is the most dangerous place on earth. Have you ever gone back and forth on a thought, mentally debating if you should do what's right or move in flesh and do what is wrong! The mind is the place where actions, emotions, and motives are birthed. People say I made that mistake because I wasn't thinking. The truth of the matter was, you were thinking, but not correctly. When you think correctly you align it with proper decision making. You truly consider the consequences of a thought that produces the action. A thought is the first step in any direction. My father would always tell us. Whatever you think on the longest becomes the strongest. Whatsoever a man thinks, so is he. Wherever you are right now in life is a reflection of your past thoughts. You are currently driving, eating, and living according to a thought.

Your thoughts become your words

Your words become your actions

Your actions become habits and habits become your destiny.

Mentally there is a daily battle. A battle that you can have the victory over. You decide to do things positively or negatively. You can choose to give in or get up. You choose to pursue or retreat. It's all a choice, but those choices breathe from how you think. You may say, how do I change the way I think? How do I change a mindset of doubt, fear, and unbelief?

Let's go to the word!!!! The scripture tells us in Philippians whatever is true, whatever is noble, whatever is right, whatever is pure, whatever is lovely, whatever is admirable—if anything is excellent or praiseworthy—think about such things. 2 Corinthians 10:5 reminds us to demolish arguments and every pretension that sets itself up against the knowledge of God taking captive every thought to make it obedient to Christ.

The word tells us to take captive of every thought. Once a thought comes you have the authority to swallow it or spit it out. It's just that serious. If you took a drink of bleach, you would immediately spit it out of your mouth because it can harm you. It could affect your inside organs and even cause death. Just as you would get rid of the bleach you must rid your mind from doubt, fear, and unbelief. These things cripple the promises of God in your life. They become toxic and leads to spiritual death. You can conquer the battle of the mind with the correct thoughts. Join me today as we pray the will of the father.

Prayer: Father it is your will that I prosper in my mind. No more mind battles; No more mind games. I take upon the mind of Christ. I take captive of every thought. This battle is won through your word. Amen.

I cause a shift in the atmosphere and I will walk in more faith and more glory than I ever have before. I am on fire for God. I make a solid decision to run after God like it is my last chance. I have no time to waste, my gifts, talents, abilities will be utilized for the kingdom.

Ramona Golphin-Webb

Day 25

Through love and Kindness

Titus 3:4-5 NIV
But when the kindness and love of God our Savior appeared, 5 he saved us, not because of righteous things we had done, but because of his mercy.

My mother is the most joyful, forgiving, and loving person I know. I never could understand how she could smile and be so happy and joyful every day!!! I did not always understand why she was so forgiving and kind either. My siblings and I would get so upset if we felt that people were getting over on her. It was to the point that I thought my mom was just gullible (with all due respect) and she liked when people got over on her. Lord forgive my ignorance!!! As I got older I began to learn what love and kindness really meant. To love meant to forgive. To be kind meant to be considerate, generous, and friendly. All these years I thought my mother was gullible in actuality she was walking in pure love and kindness. She would say, Mona, "you must love people beyond where they are, and you have to love them right where they are now." She would tell us to Trust God and love people. How can you love people beyond where they are and still love them where they are? I did not understand at that time. Now I know that meant to love a person beyond their current faults, mistakes, and wrongdoings. Even if they have done you wrong, you must love them. Then you must love them right in the mistake, the mess and in their wrong. Even when you know they are entangled, going through self-inflicted storms and battles, you need to love them. She said, "Don't walk away or give up on them even when you know that they are really the cause of their pain and storms." Mom was so right because true love and kindness can lead to repentance and a soft answer drives away wrath. It all begins to make a lot of sense to me. That is why Pastor Mary is so blessed, smiles through the rain, dances and praises God as she does. She knew an open secret. She was on a love path. The Bible declares we treat others the way we would want to be treated. That means if you want to be loved you must show and give that same love. Now I know why my mom never has a bad day. I have never seen her sad or even down. She tapped into a walk of love that overrides fear, stress, and defeat. The Joy of the lord is truly your strength. I believe that because God is love he will ask us how we exemplified his love to others. Moses received Ten Commandments from God for the people to live by. We understand that these commandments were under the law. These 10 may have been hard to follow by or hard to remember, so there are two commandments that condense them all together. Love your neighbor as yourself and love the Lord your God with all your heart, mind, and soul. When you walk in these two commandments the ten are easy. You can easily walk in love. Think about it; you would not steal or kill because you would not want that to happen to you. I hope you have learned the importance of walking in love and kindness. Choose today to walk a new path. A path that leads to freedom and kindness love in all areas of your life. Thank you, Pastor Mary, for showing me Gods Love. Let us Pray.

Prayer: Lord I thank you for your example of true love and kindness. I choose to follow that example. I ask you to forgive me of areas where I did not show your love and kindness. I change my path today. I choose to love and to show kindness. Amen.

I declare a fresh anointing of God over my life. Every sleep, dormant gift will awaken and be used for the glory of God. I decree health and wholeness Mentally, Physically, and Emotionally over my life.

Ramona Golphin-Webb

Day 26

Shhhhh, Watch Your Mouth

Luke 1:13, 18-20 NIV

But the angel said to him:" Do not be afraid, Zechariah; your prayer has been heard. Your wife Elizabeth will bear you a son, and you are to call him John.

18 Zechariah asked the angel, "How can I be sure of this? I am an old man and my wife is well along in years.

19 The angel said to him," I am Gabriel. I stand in the presence of God, and I have been sent to speak to you to tell you this good news. 20 And now you will be silent and not able to speak until the day this happens because you did not believe my words, which will come true at their appointed time.

Let us begin with a little spiritual exercise. Could you just put your pointer finger right in front of your mouth before reading this? Practice makes perfect. Shhhhhh, let us get a lesson from Zechariah.

Zechariah prayed and asked God for a son. God sends an angel to tell Zechariah that he has heard his request and has answered his prayers. The angel told him that he and his ife, Elizabeth would bare a son. The angel came and related this great news but instead of Zechariah thanking God for answering his prayer he wanted to know how this could be. Let me remind you, Elizabeth was barren and they both were older in age. You may wonder why would he ask how could it be when this was what he has prayed for?

Have you ever prayed for something and when God sends the sign of giving you just that, you go back and doubt his ability to do it?? This is exactly what Zechariah did. The very thing he prayed for was in process, but he begins to look at his situation (physically) and allowed doubt to come in. He told the angel that he was old and so was his wife. As if God wasn't aware of his age and physical capabilities. God knew everything about the situation before Zechariah even prayed for a son. God is always one step ahead. He is not expecting us to figure out how he is going do it. He may not even tell us how he is going to do it. Just consider it done. All you need to know is that if God says YES nobody can say NO! If he says it is a "GO," you can bank on it happening.

It's important to watch what we say. Zechariah learned this lesson the hard way.

"Shhhhh," Silent Now Zechariah!!!

Gabriel the angel silenced Zechariah because he doubted the answer to his own prayers. God will keep you even when you do not want to be kept. If it is his will then he will fulfill. He already knows what the future holds.

John the Baptist was born just as the angel had said. John had the spirit and power of Elijah. He was the voice that cried out in the Wilderness, Prepare ye the way of the Lord. His birth was necessary, and God knew it was best that nothing, but Faith talked while John was in the womb! The mouth of doubt was closed shut until the promise was birthed. Zechariah was mute for 9 months! What if God silenced us when we doubted what he said he was going to do! Aren't you thankful for grace?

Please remember to watch your mouth. When you pray to an almighty God, be prepared to receive that in which you have requested. Do not be afraid or worry how it is going to happen. Just receive it.

Now put your finger back over your mouth. Shhhhhhh!!! Practice makes perfect.

Speak this aloud:

I will watch the words that come out of my mouth.

My Words are powerful. They can Cost me or Pay me. I only pray the will of the father.

I will not doubt the answer he gives. I trust Gods plans even when I am not sure how he will do it His Will - He Will fulfill. Amen.

33 But seek first his kingdom and his righteousness, and all these things will be given to you as well.

Matthew 6:33 NIV

God

Family

Career

In that order

Day 27

Fear vs Faith

2 Timothy 1:7 KJV

For God has not given us a spirit of fear, but of power, and of love and a sound mind.

There are several things you would have done if you were not afraid. We tend to give up on ideas and visions because fear creeps in and challenges what we dream of doing. After today, you will never allow fear to stop you from accomplishing your dreams and goals. Let us break it down. What is fear? Fear is the anticipation of the possibility that something unpleasant could occur. The key words are a possibility and could. These two words tell us that what you may fear may not be real. It is only a possibility. Fear is the product of the choice you make. Yes!!!!! It is a choice to fear or not to fear. The danger of a dog's bite is real, but you still have to make a choice to fear it. Who says because the dog has the ability to bite that he would bite you? It is the smell of fear that triggers the bite! Could fear really be the factor that is holding you back? When you are not confident in what you believe, in your plans, or in your ideas and goals; you attract the spirit of fear. God has not given us a spirit of fear but of power, love, and a sound mind.

You have to keep the Faith, Keep it in your fears and through your tears. Faith in God is the only thing that will secure your future. It will comfort the present and allow you to look past, the past. Faith in God and his word is the ulti-mate power. It is the substance of anything you desire and want. It is the eyes of the unseen. It is an indestructible weapon. A weapon that we must use daily. It is Fears enemy! Remember, the Just shall live by faith. On the flipside, the just will die and faint when faith is lost. To believe in God is to believe in his promises. Heaven and Earth will pass away before his word goes unfulfilled. "*Faith in God is a sleeping pill at night, and an alarm clock in the morning, so work your measure of Faith.*" Have Faith in God...One day at a time.

Faith cancels out Fear.

When you fail to believe you will find an excuse to fail. You cannot base your story off of another person's story. Just because they're planned failed does not mean yours will. How will you ever know if you are too afraid to try? Once you defeat fear you have to make it a habit to continue in faith.

So, open the daycare

Sign up for college

Write the book

Pursue the business

Do not allow fear to stop you. It is only false evidence appearing to be real. Do it, even if you have to do it afraid. Take the Risk and watch God take the Rest.

Prayer: God I thank you for delivering me from all fears. Your word tells me that you have given me power, love, and a sound mind. No longer will I fear. I will finish, and I will conquer. Amen.

But remember the LORD your God, for it is he who gives you the ability to produce wealth, and so confirms his covenant, which he swore to your ancestors, as it is today.

Deuteronomy 8:18NIV

Day 28

I AM A CHAMPION

Today I want to awaken the Champion in you. The Bible says that we are more than conquers through Christ Jesus. We can do all thing through Christ Jesus; in him, we live, we move and have our being.

Let us kick-start the day with this Champion Confession. Believe what you say and confess it with **BOLDNESS.**

GOD BRINGS OUT THE CHAMPION IN ME!

I KNOW WHO I AM!

I CAN'T BE STOPPED!

I CAN'T FAIL!

I ALWAYS WIN!

I AM SUCCESS!

I AM THE BEST!

GOD IS MY COACH!

HOLY SPIRIT IS MY MENTOR!

GREATNESS DWELLS IN ME!

I WAS CREATED TO WIN!

ENDURE!

TAKE OVER!

BRING CHANGE!

I AM A CHAMPION!

No matter how you feel or what you may be faced with today; be encouraged in knowing that you are a winner. Hold your head up high because you have what it takes. You are a Champion!

Day 29

Forgive and Live

Matthew 6:14:15 NIV

14 For if you forgive other people when they sin against you, your heavenly Father will also forgive you. 15 But if you do not forgive others their sins, your Father will not forgive your sins.

Matthew 18:21-22NIV

21Then Peter came to Jesus and asked, "Lord, how many times shall I forgive my brother or sister who sins against me? Up to seven times?"

22 Jesus answered, "I tell you, not seven times, but seventy-seven times."

Have you ever been in a place where you knew you should forgive, you even tried to forgive but it just seemed like you could not let what happened to go? Or maybe you were so hurt that you did not desire to forgive at all? Did it make you feel better or safer not to forgive?

Let us talk about it.

Forgiveness is very important. Your entire being is affected when you hold un-forgiveness in your heart. Un-forgiveness causes mental, emotional, and physical sickness. Your emotions are linked to your mental and physical health. When you hold unforgiveness it creates a hole in you. The branch of bitterness begins to attach itself as well. Bitterness eats at you from the inside out. It sours within you and holds you back from loving again, trying again, and moving forward. Un-forgiveness has many more branches. Anger, rejection, resentment, and grudges are just to name a few. It is deeper than what has happened to you, it is important not to let what has happened to you work through you. It is not that what has happened to you was right or deserving, but regardless of the event or activity un-forgiveness is a choice. You make the choice to hold it within or to release it. Not only should you forgive others, but you must forgive yourself. We have all done things that we never imagined we would. We all have gotten ourselves involved in situations that have made us feel guilty and condemned. The enemy wants us to never forgive ourselves, so he can open the doors of guilt, shame, and condemnation. It is a trap to hold you back. Do not punish yourself any longer, just forgive!!!! Forgive you! Forgiveness is for you! We have been taught that we should forgive to free the other person and that may happen, but when you make a choice to forgive, it is you that receive 100%Freedom.

How do you know that you have forgiven? When you see the person or hear their name, that feeling will not rise from within you. We all know the feeling I am referring to. For an example, if you see them in Walmart on the bread aisle, and you need bread, but you turn and go in the other direction, maybe there is something still there because when you have completely forgiven and handed the outcome to God you have the freedom to move as you please. When un-forgiveness is in control, it controls your when what, and how. If you need bread, do not lap Walmart three times trying to avoid a person. Let it go. The Bible declares that we forgive a person 70 x 7. This means after the 490th time then maybe you can hold them in un-forgiveness! Until then, forgiveness is a commandment. Remember that if we do not forgive others our father in Heaven will not forgive us.

Now is the time to forgive. It is time to let it go and move forward. It's been holding you back far too long. Are you ready?

Let us pray!

Prayer: Lord I release every hurt and disappointment that has caused me to walk in un-forgiveness. I choose to forgive every person that has hurt me, abused me, and rejected me. I forgive myself. I forgive every event and situation from my childhood up into my present. I no longer hold it against them, myself, or you. I walk in love for you are love. I am free. Amen.

Day 30

The WAY Maker

Exodus 14:16-18 KJV

16 But Lift up thy rod, and stretch out thine hand over the sea, and divide it; and the children of Israel shall go on dry ground through the midst of the sea.**17** And I, behold, I will harden the hearts of the Egyptians, and they shall follow them: and I will get me honor upon Pharaoh, and all his host, upon his host ,upon his chariots, and upon his horse-men.**18** And the Egyptians shall know that I am the LORD, when I have gotten me honor upon Pharaoh, upon his chari-ots, and upon his horsemen.

I remember reading the story of the Israelites crossing the Red Sea. Moses was told by God to tell Pharaoh to Let his people go. After several plagues and the death of his son, Pharaoh finally agreed. The Israelites were on their way with no worries or concerns until (BOOM) they were confronted with The Red Sea. Not only did the sea appear, but they also noticed that Pharaoh and his army decided they wanted them back in slavery, so he and his army chased behind them. The Israelites were surrounded, and it looked as if there was no way out! Have you ever felt like this?

Many of them began to complain and doubt ever seeing the promise land because of the unexpected Red Sea in front of them. Just when they thought the past was over they looked back and there it appeared. Fear crept in and the Israelites thought it was no way out. This is exactly what we do when something unexpected pops up in our path. It seems like all is well and then (BOOM) A negative report (BOOM) job lays you off (Boom after Boom!) It really looked like it was no way out, over or in. Has it ever got so bad that you felt you would never reach the promises of God? I got great news, I am here to let you know that even though a Red Sea circumstance may be in the way, God is a way maker. Where there seems to be no way, he creates a way. It does not matter what pops up from your past or what obstacle you are currently facing. God never comes too early or too late. He will come through for you at the right time.

Moses stretched out his rod and the sea began to part. The Israelites walked over on dry land. God performed a miracle right in the face of Pharaoh and his men. As soon as the Israelites crossed over, The Red Sea came back down, and

Pharaoh and his army drowned. Not even your past will be able to prevent you from his promises. God is the same yesterday today and forever. Just as he parted the sea he is moving things out of your way so that you can walk into his promises. God is a way maker. Do not worry about what is behind you, or what is in the way. Keep the faith and watch him make a way! Let us pray.

Prayer: God you are my way maker. You are a miracle worker. My past is behind me never to enslave me again. I will see the promises you have for me. I will not doubt but continue to trust your word. Thank you for making way for me. Amen

Champion Faith

I have the FAITH to Fight
The Faith to Finish

For The lord is my Light, My Salvation
Whom shall I fear?
The Lord is the strength of my life!
In what situation should I be afraid!

The Champion in me Shall Arise, Pursue,
Conquer, and WIN!
I will finish STRONG! I am A Champion!!

Ramona Golphin-Webb

Day 31
Give Thanks

1Thessalonians 5:18 NIV

Give thanks in all circumstances; for this is God's will for you in Christ Jesus.

I have one special Facebook friend that post this quote every day. "Did you tell God Thank you for waking you up this Morning? When I would see Mr. Ed Veasley post no matter what time of the day it was, I would whisper," Thank you God for another day.

Another day is another opportunity and another reason to say thank you. What if you woke up tomorrow and all you had was what you thanked God for yesterday! It is something to think about. We teach small children to say thank you, but then we forget to say it. We take for granted the air in our lungs, the activity of our limbs, food on our tables and clothes on our backs. We may not eat steak every day but at least our bellies are pleased with something. It is a blessing to even have an appetite. Sometimes we get so caught up in what we have or our gifts that we forget the giver. Remember that real appreciation and gratitude comes from the heart.

There is a story in the Bible about 10 lepers. Jesus was on his way to Jerusalem and he encountered 10 lepers. Jesus healed all 10 of them, but only one came back to say thank you. Jesus asked, "Weren't there 9 more that was healed?? But only one came back to say thank you?" He then told the thankful leper that his faith and thankfulness has made him whole. There is always more in store when you are thankful. You can be healed, or you can become completely whole. It all depends on your thankfulness.

My father told the story of a young boy who was promised a new bike from his dad. The dad intended on getting this new bike in a few months. Every day the little boy would tell his dad how thankful he was for his new bike. The father was so moved that he went and bought the bike the next day. Thankfulness always moves the heart of a giver. God is pleased when we give him thanks. Thankfulness speeds up the manifestation. Practice thanking God in advanced and watch what happens. In all things, for all things Give thanks. It should not be forced or taken. Think back on the goodness of the lord and take a moment to reflect on his mercy, love, protection, provision, and grace. We have more than enough to thank him for. Let us take a moment to thank him.

Thank you, God, for health and strength.

Thank you for a sound mind.

Thank you for my sight and hearing.

Thank you for my family and friends.

Thank you for making ways and opening doors when there was no way.

Thank you for healing my mind and body.

Thank you for sending your son to love me, die for me and for redeeming me from every curse.

Thank you for another breathe another day and another opportunity to say

Thank you. Amen.

I pray this book has been a blessing to you. 31 days have passed, and they are now gone, but allow the word of God to remain in your heart. Go back and read this book over and over again. I am sure you will discover new revelation every time you pick it up.

It is now up to you to take the word in this devotional and apply it to your life.

It is the will of God that you Succeed, WIN, Overcome and Triumph over every circumstance.

Remember, you are the advertisement for the Kingdom. You have what it takes! God injected everything in you that you will need to get the job done. It's locked up on the inside of you. Discover your purpose and display it to the World. We need it and God is counting on you. For his namesake, has he prepared you for Success! Now FINISH STRONG!

Don't give up ... just take God's Word
One day at a Time
#BeEncouraged

Ramona Golphin -Webb

One Day at a Time

About the Author

Ramona Golphin-Webb is a walking advertisement for the Kingdom of God. She is the spokeswoman for this generation. Ramona is a University of Memphis Graduate and a Paul Michell the Hair School of Memphis graduate. She has worked as a Medical social worker in Hospice, as a Social service director for Nursing Homes, and a case manager for the Mentally ill.

Ramona presently is a hair stylist and owner of The Mona Nissi Salon in Blytheville, Arkansas. She is a wife and mother of two blessed children. Ramona attends Frontline Family Outreach Ministries, also located in Blytheville, Arkansas. She plays the keyboard, drums, and Ministers through song and speaking. Her mission is to encourage and motivate others to trust God and to never give up on the plan he has for their lives.

Made in the USA
Columbia, SC
25 October 2024

44686929R00063